JASPER

& SCRUFF

THE
COOL
CAT
CLUB

tiger tales

5 River Road, Suite 128, Wilton, CT 06897
Published in the United States 2020
Originally published in Great Britain 2019
by the Little Tiger Group
Text and illustrations copyright © 2019 Nicola Colton
ISBN-13: 978-1-68010-460-8
ISBN-10: 1-68010-460-8
Printed in China
STP/1800/0288/1019
All rights reserved
10 9 8 7 6 5 4 3 2 1

For more insight and activities, visit us at
www.tigertalesbooks.com

by Nicola Colton

JASPER
& SCRUFF

THE Cool CAT Club

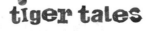

tiger tales

Jasper was the type of cat
who knew what he liked.

He liked living on the top floor of
a grand apartment building, which
was so fancy, it even had a doorman.

He liked having a large bookcase
full of impressive books, which
he had arranged by color.

He liked his wardrobe, which
contained bow ties in every
pattern imaginable.

But there was **one thing** that Jasper did not have—the *right* friends. More than anything, he wanted to be a member of

The Sophisticats,

the society for exceptional felines.

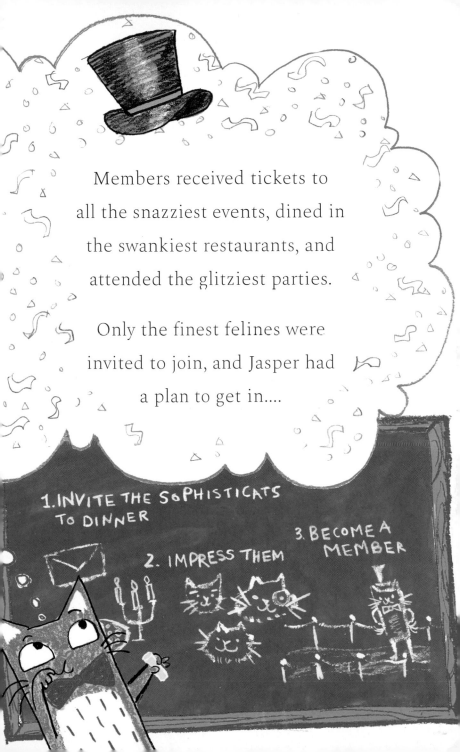

Members received tickets to all the snazziest events, dined in the swankiest restaurants, and attended the glitziest parties.

Only the finest felines were invited to join, and Jasper had a plan to get in....

1. INVITE THE SOPHISTICATS TO DINNER

2. IMPRESS THEM

3. BECOME A MEMBER

Jasper waited ... and waited ...
for The Sophisticats to reply
to his invitation.

He was ironing his bow tie one
morning when something sharp
hit him on the back of the head.

Floating to the ground was a
handsome envelope with his name
printed on it in brilliant gold.

He picked it up and carefully opened it.

The Sophisticats

Dear Jasper,

The Sophisticats have accepted your dinner party invitation. We shall be gracing you with our presence on Saturday at 7 p.m. sharp. We expect only the finest dining and top-notch entertainment. Everything must be absolutely purrfect if you wish to become a member of our rather exclusive club.

Cattiest regards,

The Sophisticats

Jasper checked his planner. "But that's only two days away!" he panicked. With no time to waste, Jasper got to work....

12

He polished the silverware until it gleamed. He dusted his art collection. He took down all the recipe books from his bookcase. He wrote a shopping list. He *even* took a bath.

The morning of the dinner party arrived.
Picking up his shopping basket, Jasper
headed off to Snootington High Street.

GIOVANNI'S DELI,

30

ERY

BERNARD'S CANDLES

At the deli, Jasper counted
the holes in the cheese.

"No, this will not do at all.
Poke more holes in this Gouda,"
he told the shopkeeper.
"And I'll also have a wedge of your
stinkiest, bluest, tangiest Stilton."

At the fish market, he measured the fish.

He watched the bread rise at the bakery.

He walked around sniffing, poking, and
squeezing things in the Fine Foods store
before putting them in his basket.
Only the best would do.

On his way home, he took a shortcut through the park. Suddenly, he heard a peculiar noise behind him. A kind of panting sound....

He turned around.

There on the path, staring up at him, was something he did not like one bit.

It was a puppy.

Jasper shuddered. Dogs were bad enough, but puppies…. They were the opposite of everything he liked— noisy, unruly, and worst of all, messy. He could not stand them!

The puppy tilted his head and gave Jasper a hopeful look. Then he leaped into Jasper's arms and gave him a BIG, SLOPPY LICK.

"Get off me!" Jasper cried,
putting down his bags and
wiping the drool from his
face with a silk hanky.

"Hello! I'm Scruff,"
the puppy yapped,
wagging his tail excitedly.
"What's your name?"

"Not interested," said Jasper.
He picked up his bags
and started to walk away.

Scruff followed.

"Not interested?

That's a funny name!

Do you like the park?

It's my favorite place!

It's great for games.

Do you want to play fetch?"

Before Jasper had the chance to reply,
the puppy leaped into a nearby flower bed.

He returned with a drool-soaked ball,
which he dropped at Jasper's feet.

"Great idea," said Jasper. He picked
up the slobbery ball with his hanky
and threw it as far as he could.

"Fetch!"

The puppy bounded off to get the ball...

...and Jasper quickly made his
way back to his apartment.
He closed the door with a click.

"My goodness," he muttered. "That
creature got mud everywhere. Still, at
least I got rid of—"

Jasper looked down. The bags
of groceries slid from his paws
and thudded onto the floor.

To Jasper's astonishment, Scruff had managed to follow him all the way home.

"You again? How did you get past the doorman *and* into my apartment?" he asked weakly.

"Hello! That was fun!" said Scruff, wagging his tail. He dropped the ball at Jasper's feet. "Do you want to play again?"

Jasper thought for a moment.
He picked up the slobbery ball
with his hanky.

Then he stepped out into the hallway
and hurled it down the stairs.

Scruff scampered after the ball, and
Jasper followed quickly behind.

"Let's play another game," Jasper said as the ball bounced down the front steps and rolled off down the street. "How about hide-and-seek? You go back to the park and count to a thousand."

"Aren't you coming, too?" asked Scruff.

"Um, yes," said Jasper. "I just need to grab my coat."

"Okay, but you'll have to think of a good hiding place," said Scruff. "I'm great at hide-and-seek."

Jasper rolled his eyes as he watched Scruff bound off toward the park.

Then he headed back upstairs.

Jasper placed the shopping bags on the
kitchen table, put on his chef's hat, and
opened up a recipe book.

But as he reached for the eggs,
he realized they were *broken*.

"How am I going to make my Salmon Soufleé now?" Jasper wondered aloud as he wiped the goo from his paw.

Sighing, Jasper erased Salmon Soufleé from the menu and wrote Salmon Surprise. He would just have to make something up.

He zoomed around the kitchen, chopping, stirring, and sniffing. Finally, with the soup bubbling in the pot, the fish in the oven, and the cake iced, he set the table and lit the candles. He had just started to fold a napkin into a swan when—

Ding-Dong!

"They're here!" Jasper jumped.

There was no time for swans.
He straightened his bow tie
and opened the door.

"Lady Catterly, how wonderful to see y—"

"Yes, yes," she said. "Now, where's the
dining room? I'm *positively* famished."
She slung her fur coat at Jasper.

"Um, right through here.
Please make yourself at home."

"I'm parched," Lady Catterly said,
seating herself at the head of the
table. "Run along now and fetch me
your best Sparkling Catnip Juice."

She gave her crumpled
napkin a catty glance
and scribbled something
in her notebook.

SNAP
SNAP

But before Jasper could reach the kitchen, the doorbell rang again.

Ding-Dong!

"Reginald! Oswald! How splendid to see you b—"

42

"Jasper, my good man," Reginald said, rubbing his paws together as he strode into the hallway. "There's a chill in the air. Get me a hot chocolate, quick as you can!"

"Make mine a vanilla milkshake with a cherry on top," said Oswald, following behind.

"Chop, chop!" Oswald threw his cane at Jasper, hitting him on the nose.

"Ouch!" Jasper yelped. "I mean, come into the dining room...."

"Darling, I am still waiting for my drink," Lady Catterly called as they entered.

"Be with you in just a moment," said Jasper, bowing low.

Jasper hurried into the kitchen to prepare the drinks. He poured some Sparkling Catnip Juice into his finest crystal glass.

He heated up a pot of milk and stirred in some melted chocolate before tipping the mixture into a fancy mug.

Then he whipped some cream until his arm ached and spooned it on top, followed by marshmallows and chocolate shavings.

He scooped ice cream into a blender, added a splash of milk, and blended it until it became a thick, frothy milkshake. He poured it into a tall glass and topped it with a cherry.

He placed all three drinks very, very carefully onto a silver tray.

He'd just stepped out into the
hallway when he stumbled over
something soft and *scruffy*.
The tray flew up into the air...

...and landed on the floor
with a tremendous *crash*.

Jasper stared down at the mess in
disbelief. A slobbery ball rolled across
the floor and stopped by his feet.

"Found you!" panted Scruff.
"Good hiding place! I searched all
over the park, but you weren't there."

Jasper let out a long sigh. *How did that puppy get in again?* But there was no time for questions.

"Shh!" said Jasper, picking up Scruff and putting him in the bathroom. "Let's play the quiet game. You stay in here and be quiet for the rest of the evening."

"Oooh, a new game!" said Scruff.
"I love games! Is there a prize?"

"Um, yes, something good to eat,"
whispered Jasper.

He closed the bathroom door firmly
behind him and reached for his hanky.

"What was that
awful noise?"
cried Lady Catterly.
"And where is my
catnip juice?"

"Where's my hot
chocolate?"
whined Reginald.

"Hurry up and be quick about it—I need my milkshake," moaned Oswald.

"Be with you in a moment!" called Jasper. "I just had a slight mishap."

"I see," said Lady Catterly.
"Mishaps are not something
The Sophisticats approve of."

Jasper quickly remade his guests' drinks and carried them into the dining room.

"Finally," said Lady Catterly.

"About time," said Reginald.

Buuuurrrp! went Oswald.

Jasper brought out
the first course.

"May I present, Creamy Chowder
with Catnip Croutons," he said,
puffing out his chest.

Lady Catterly took a sip and handed
the bowl back to Jasper. "Ugh, this is
very bland. It needs more seasoning."

"Much too watery," said Reginald.
"Blend it with some cream."

"That was barely a mouthful," said
Oswald after guzzling it down in
one gulp. "Fetch me some more!"

Jasper gathered their bowls
and hurried back into the kitchen
to fix the soup.

His guests tasted their soup for the
second time. "Passable," they said.

Jasper brought out the next course.
*How can they possibly find anything wrong
with my Salmon Surprise?* he thought.

"Too many bones," said Lady Catterly.

"Too chewy," said Reginald.

"Noh 'nuff saush," said Oswald,
his cheeks bulging with food.

Jasper was beginning to wonder if joining The Sophisticats was worth all this trouble. "Of course. I will fix your dishes right away," he muttered.

As the cats dug into their second helping, Jasper crossed his fingers. He was so jittery that he had barely touched his own food.

"Just about edible," said Lady Catterly as the others licked their plates clean.

Jasper hoped he could turn things around with his famous Salted Caramel Cake. *Everyone loves that!* he told himself as he took the empty plates to the kitchen.

But as he stepped into the room, he let out a horrified gasp. The caramel buttercream had disappeared, and the cake was now covered in a fine coating of hair and drool.

Next to the cake stood Scruff,
panting happily.

"Hello! I was silent forever, so
I thought the game was over,"
said Scruff. "I found the prize!
It's yummy!"

"What have you done? My beautif—"
Jasper began. Then a smile spread
across his face as he thought about
his guests' behavior so far.

"Let's see what they have to say
about dessert," he said.

He took a piece of rope from a drawer and looped it around Scruff's leg. "I'm sorry, Scruff, but I need you to stay put until my guests are gone," Jasper told the puppy as he tied the other end of the rope to the table.

"Oh, okay," said Scruff. "Is this a new game?"

"Um, yes," said Jasper as he closed the door.

Jasper brought the hairy disaster of a cake to the table and set it down with a flourish.

"Dessert is served!"

"What *exactly* is this?" said Lady Catterly. "It's a frightful mess!"

"It's Gateau à la *Scruff*," said Jasper. "Haven't you heard of it? It's the Queen of Belgium's favorite, you know."

"Of course I've heard of it! Gateau à la Scruff, yes," she replied, taking a big bite.

"Mmm…. A fond favorite of mine, too," said Reginald. "It's served at *all* the fashionable parties."

"Why, I had it just the other day," said Oswald.

"Of course you did," said Jasper.

"And remind me again, what are these
stringy pieces?" asked Lady Catterly,
holding up one of Scruff's hairs.

"Oh, that's finely spun sugar,"
said Jasper. "It's made by the
best confectioners in Belgium.
Very exclusive *and* expensive."

"*Delicious*," said Lady Catterly.

"Very pleasing and wonderfully, um, moist," agreed Reginald.

"Just as good as the last time I had it," said Oswald.

"I'm delighted you like it," said Jasper. "Now, it's time for the entertainment."

He seated himself at the piano and began to play his favorite tune.

"Too slow," said Lady Catterly,
drumming her claws on the table.

"Borrrinnnng," said Reginald
with a yawn.

"Play us something more jazzy.
Chop chop!" said Oswald,
throwing his fork at Jasper's head.

As Jasper's eyes began to focus again, he
noticed that Scruff was now under the
table, chasing his ball in circles. The rope
Jasper had tied him up with was trailing
behind him, wrapping around and around
the guests' feet.

Jasper finished his tune and bowed.

"Well, I think we have seen and heard quite enough, Jasper," said Lady Catterly. "And I am not at all convinced that you are Sophisticats material."

"I agree." Reginald nodded. "Jasper is not up to snuff."

"Indeed," said Oswald. "And if we leave now, we can make the show at the Velvet Theater."

They stood up to go....

Splat!

Lady Catterly landed face
first in the remaining cake.

Crash!

Reginald stumbled into
the table and knocked
over one of the candles,
setting his hat on fire.

Boing!

Oswald bounced off the couch and found himself swinging from the chandelier by the seat of his pants.

"My fur is all matted with cake!"
wailed Lady Catterly.

"My hat has melted!" gasped Reginald.

"I'm going to fall!" cried Oswald.

There was a loud ripping sound
and he landed bottom first in
a bowl of cream.

Scruff appeared from under
the table, wagging his tail.

"A puppy!" they yowled together.

"I can't believe you let one of these disgusting beasts in the house!" said Lady Catterly. "Mark my words—you will NEVER, *EVER* be a member of The Sophisticats!"

"I second that," said Reginald.

"Yes, I ... um, quite agree," said
Oswald, blushing as he tried to hide
the hole in the back of his pants.

"Well, I can't think of anything
worse than being a member of The
Sophisticats," said Jasper. "And he's
not a beast. His name is Scruff."

"Scruff?" said Lady Catterly in a faint voice. "Like the cake?"

"Oh, yes!" Jasper grinned. "Scruff was a huge help with the cake."

"Scruff … helped?" she said, clutching her throat.

Reginald and Oswald stood, mouths open, turning a sickly green.

Jasper nodded. "He did a great job of licking off all the buttercream."

The three cats stumbled over each other as they hurried out the door.

Jasper could still hear their screeches echoing down the street as he untangled Scruff.

"Well, it was, um, interesting meeting you, Scruff," said Jasper, showing him out. "Now I must go and clean up. Time for you to head home."

"Okay," said the puppy, his eyes large and watery. "Well, then.... 'Bye."

Jasper sat down at the piano and
breathed a sigh of relief. He'd had
a lucky escape, thanks to Scruff.
Those cats were horrible! So why did
he have a funny feeling in his tummy?

PLONK!

Jasper hit several keys at once.
Had he been just as horrible to Scruff?
He ran to the door and flung it open.

"*Scruff!*" he called.

"Hello," said Scruff in a small voice.

"Oh," said Jasper. He looked down
to see the puppy sitting there.
"You're still here."

"I don't have anywhere to go,"
said Scruff.

"You don't have a home?"

"No ... not really," said Scruff.
"I've been sleeping in the park."

"Well, there's still a lot of food left,"
said Jasper. "Maybe you could do me
a *big* favor and help me finish it."
He flicked his tail encouragingly
toward the door.

"*Yummy!*" said Scruff,
and he bounded inside.

As Jasper prepared the food, he could
hear Scruff moving things around in the
living room. Swish! Thud!

Puzzled, he poked his head
around the kitchen door.

"Um, Scruff?" said Jasper as he watched
the puppy drag a large cushion off the
couch. "Feel free to make yourself at
home. But what you are doing?"

"It's a surprise," panted Scruff.
"Come back in ten minutes."
He dragged another cushion
off the couch. Swish! Thud!

Jasper folded his arms to stop
himself from putting the cushions
back in place. "Well, okay...."

When Jasper returned with a tray piled high with Salmon Surprise and a freshly baked cake, he was met with a surprising sight.

"Oh, Scruff!" he gasped. "It's wonderful!"

Scruff had turned the cushions
and blankets into a cozy fort.

"Why don't you come inside?"
said Scruff.

Somehow, Jasper thought as they talked and ate, *my cooking tastes better than ever before. And I can't remember the last time I had so much fun....*

With their tummies full of food, Jasper and Scruff were both soon rubbing their eyes and yawning.

"Why don't you stay with me, Scruff?"
asked Jasper. "I have plenty of room.
You can sleep in here for now until
we get you your own bed."

"Thank you!" Scruff leaped into
Jasper's arms and gave him a
BIG, SLOPPY LICK!

Scruff curled up on some cushions, and
Jasper covered him with a blanket.

"Good night, Scruff," he whispered.

Smiling, Jasper tiptoed across the
room and turned off the light.

He had found the
right type of friend after all.